KINGS & QUEENS
BOOK I
1,000 ~ 1399
THE MILLENNIUM SERIES

by
John Guy

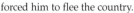

AETHELRED THE UNREADY (978-1016)

Aethelred was a weak monarch who tried to buy off the Vikings by paying them money, known as the Danegeld, raised from taxes. It was an unpopular and ineffective measure that forced him to flee the country.

A DANISH KING

Following the death of Alfred, England remained at war with the Viking invaders for the next 150 years. Peace came under the strong and wise leadership of Canute, a Dane, who was crowned king of England, Denmark and Norway (1016-35). Canute was said to be so powerful that he could command the waves, a claim he vehemently denied, as shown above.

LINE OF SUCCESSION

Saxon & Danish Kings

Ecgberht - 827-839
Aethelwulf - 839-866
Aethelred I - 866-871
Alfred the Great - 871-899
Edward the Elder - 899-925
Athelstan- 925-939
Edmund I - 939-946
Eadred I - 946-959
Eadgar the Peaceable - 959-975
Edward the Martyr - 975-978
Aethelred II - 978-1013 & 1014-1016
Sweyn (Dane) - 1013-1014
Edmund Ironside (Dane) - 1016
Canute (Dane) - 1016-1035
Harold Harefoot (Dane) - 1035-1040
Harthacanute (Dane) - 1040-1042
Edward the Confessor - 1042-1066
Harold II - 1066

EARLY KINGS

SAXON & DANISH KINGS (up to 1066)

*U*ntil the 9th century, Britain was a divide land with many separate kingdoms. The area we now know as England was first unified under the rule of Ecgberht (827-39) but peace did not last. Alfred the Great finally unit the nation and ruled over all England from 886 until his death in 899. Succession to the throne in Saxon England was far from being a formalit passing automatically from father to eldest son. The crown was frequently wrested by acts of violence on the battlefield or even by murder. For a brief period in the early 11th century England was ruled by Danish kings. In 1066 the Normans (or Norse-men) who were also of Scandinavian descent, claimed the English crown. They brought stability to the throne and from then on began the modern syste of numbering the monarchs.

EADGAR THE PEACEABLE

Eadgar the Peaceable came to the throne in 959 and the following year installed Dunstan as Archbishop of Canterbu He was known as the 'Peaceable' because his reign was one of prospe and relative peace with the Vikings. Eadgar also divided the shires into smaller units of administration known as hundreds, each with its own court.

ECGBERHT (827-39)

First King of All England
In 802 Ecgberht became King of Wessex, which soon became the most powerful of the Saxon kingdoms. In 827 the other six kings swore allegiance to him and he became the first true king of a united England.

 ARCHITECTURE   ARTS & LITERATURE   EXPLORATION   FAMOUS BATTLE

EDWARD-A PIOUS KING (1042-66)

Edward (above), known as the Confessor because of his pious nature, proved to be a strong king, though his preference for Norman advisers incurred the wrath of the Saxon nobility and led, eventually, to the conquest of England by the Normans.

✝ **THE VENERABLE BEDE**

The first proper English history book, the 'Ecclesiastical History of the English Nation', was written by Bede (673-735) a Saxon monk from the monasteries of Monkwearmouth and Jarrow, in the kingdom of Northumbria.

📖 **ANGLO SAXON CHRONICLE**

In 891 Alfred the Great instigated the compilation of the Anglo-Saxon Chronicle in an attempt to record the history of his newly unified nation. Written in Anglo-Saxon, instead of Latin, it gives a brief social and political history of England from before the Roman occupation to the Norman conquest.

🏛 **WESTMINSTER ABBEY**

The original Westminster Abbey was founded in the 7th century and rebuilt by Edward the Confessor between 1052-65. Rebuilt again by Henry III after 1272 additions were made right up to the 18th century. The Benedictine abbey itself was dissolved by Henry VIII in 1540 but the magnificent church remains. Most English monarchs have been crowned at the abbey and many are buried there.

ALFRED THE GREAT (871-99)

Alfred succeeded to the throne of Wessex in 871 and immediately set about reducing the Danish threat. It is whilst Alfred was in hiding in Somerset that he is supposed to have burned the cakes left in his charge, whilst plotting against the Danes. Despite early defeats, he eventually forced the Danes to sign a treaty at Wedmore in 878 confining them to an area north of the Wash, known as Danelaw. In 886 Alfred finally defeated the Danes at London and was recognised as King of all England.

KING OFFA (757-96)

For long, the most powerful of the Saxon kingdoms was Mercia, under the able rule of Offa. The Celtic people of what is now Wales, to the west, were a constant threat so Offa had a huge defensive earthwork, known as Offa's Dyke, constructed to protect his lands, much of which still survives today.

The Seven Kingdoms

Scotland

Northumbria

Occupied by Britons

Boundaries of Kingdoms

North Wales

Mercia

North Folk
East Anglia
South Folk

Essex

Wessex

Kent

West Wales

Sussex

THE KINGDOMS OF ENGLAND

From the departure of the Romans until about 827 England was divided into seven separate kingdoms, known as the Heptarchy, as shown on this map. Scotland, Wales and Ireland were also separate kingdoms in their own right.

🏛 GOVERNMENT   ⚕ HEALTH & MEDICINE   ⚖ JUSTICE   ✝ RELIGION   📜 SCIENCE

THE BATTLE OF HASTINGS
CLAIMANTS TO THE THRONE

THE INVASION FLEET

During the course of 1066 Duke William assembled a huge fleet of ships to transport his army of 4000 infantry and 3000 cavalry, together with their horses and supplies, across the Channel. He landed at Pevensey Bay, on the Sussex coast, and then moved on to Hastings.

HASTINGS CASTLE

William transported prefabricated timber panels in his invasion fleet, which he used to construct a temporary castle on the cliffs at Hastings. The Bayeux Tapestry shows clearly the Normans digging ditches and constructing the mound for this, one of the first motte and bailey castles in England.

Edward the Confessor was half-Norman and until the age of 35, lived with his mother in Normandy. After he became king he often surrounded himself with Norman advisers and in 1051 he promised the English throne to Duke William of Normandy. On his deathbed, however, Edward stated that his brother-in-law Harold Godwinson, Earl of Wessex, should be king. Harold had previously (in 1064) sworn allegiance to Duke William, so when he was crowned king William declared his intention to invade England and take the throne by force.

BATTLE ABBEY

Following his victor William vowed to b an abbey on the site the battle. Begun so after, it was not completed until 109 seven years after th Conqueror's death. Greatly extended in later centuries, muc of the abbey still survives today.

HAROLD GODWINSON

Harold was the son of Godwin, Earl of Wessex, whose sister Edith married the king, Edward the Confessor. An ongoing dispute eventually led, in 1051, to the Godwin family being banished from England. They were restored to their estates the following year and in 1053 Harold became the king's chief adviser. He persuaded Edward to renege on his promise to pass the crown to Duke William and had himself proclaimed king on Edward's death on 5th January 1066.

ARCHITECTURE   ARTS & LITERATURE   EXPLORATION   FAMOUS BATTLE

📖 BAYEUX TAPESTRY

Odo, Bishop of Bayeux and half brother of Duke William, is believed to have commissioned the Bayeux Tapestry, a huge needlework tableau (shown far left and below) depicting the events leading up to, and following, the Battle of Hastings, as part of the victory celebrations. Several scenes from the tapestry are shown here.

💣 BATTLE OF STAMFORD BRIDGE

William's invasion consisted of a two-pronged attack. While he slipped across the Channel unopposed, Harold Hardrada, king of Norway, launched an attack in the north. Harold Godwinson (of England) defeated the Norwegians at the Battle of Stamford Bridge in Yorkshire. The weary Saxons then had to march 250 miles south to meet William and the Normans encamped in Sussex.

THE BATTLE

The battle took place on 14th October 1066 about six miles north of Hastings on an escarpment known as Senlac Hill. Both armies were evenly matched, though the Saxons were tired from their long march south following the Battle of Stamford Bridge.
The Saxons occupied the top of the ridge and successfully held off the Norman advances. Late in the day, William ordered his men to feign a retreat. The Saxons gave chase and lost the advantage of the high ground, leaving them at the mercy of the Norman archers and cavalry. The Normans were victorious and though Harold sustained a fatal injury, it is not now certain that he actually died on the battlefield. The above is a late 15th century illustration of the Battle of Hastings.

WILLIAM OF NORMANDY

The Normans, or 'Norsemen', were originally Vikings who settled in an area of northern France in the early 10th century. They built up a powerful domain, ruled by a duchy, rivalling the power of the king of France. William was the illegitimate son of Robert, Duke of Normandy, and he succeeded to the dukedom in 1035 when only 8 years old. He greatly extended his empire to much of western Europe and is said never to have engaged in a fight he did not win.

vides England into two,
with Alfred as overlord.
886
Alfred becomes accepted as king of all England.

890
Alfred forms first fleet of warships to ward off Viking attacks.
891
Anglo-Saxon

Chronicle begun.
899
Death of Alfred the Great.
911
Rollo, Viking leader, is created Count of

Normandy by French king.
925
Athelstan becomes king of all England.
1016
Canute becomes

first Danish king of England.
1042
Edward the Confessor accedes to the throne.

🏛 GOVERNMENT   ⚱ HEALTH & MEDICINE   ⚖ JUSTICE   ✝ RELIGION   📘 SCIENCE

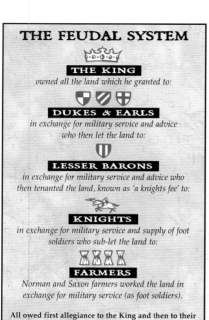

THE FEUDAL SYSTEM

THE KING
owned all the land which he granted to:

DUKES & EARLS
in exchange for military service and advice who then let the land to:

LESSER BARONS
in exchange for military service and advice who then tenanted the land, known as 'a knights fee' to:

KNIGHTS
in exchange for military service and supply of foot soldiers who sub-let the land to:

FARMERS
Norman and Saxon farmers worked the land in exchange for military service (as foot soldiers).

All owed first allegiance to the King and then to their respective overlords, to whom they also paid rents.

THE FEUDAL SYSTEM

One of the first things William did on becoming king was to reorganise the governmental structure of England with the introduction of the feudal system. Basically, all land was held by the king and sub-tenanted to his most loyal lords. They in turn sub-let their holdings and so on, down to tenant farmers. All owed allegiance to their immediate overlord, and ultimately the king, who could call upon them at any time to do military service.

📖 THE DOMESDAY BOOK

In 1085 William ordered the compilation of a great survey of his newly conquered land. Completed in just one year and covering most of the country, it records in minute detail the land ownership and uses of almost every village and estate. The population of England at that time was recorded as two million. Compiled in two huge volumes, the Domesday Book (right) still exists today.

THE ROYAL FORESTS

In medieval times the word 'forest' simply meant an area set aside f hunting and included woodland and open land. By the end of the 12 century about one-third of England had been designated royal fores One of the first of these was the New Forest in Hampshire in 1079. Severe forest laws were introduced to protect the game for hunting

THE HARRYING OF THE NORTH

In the years immediately following the Conquest several rebellions br out against Norman rule, the most serious being in the north of Engla William responded with a 'scorched earth' policy, burning and layin waste huge areas of the north to quash the rebellion.

MOTTE & BAILEY CASTLES

William was able to hold down his newly conquered lands in England w the help of castles, the private fortified residences of his barons. Early castles were constructed of earth and timber for speed and consisted of mound, or motte, surmounted by a wooden tower, with a courtyard, o bailey, attached, the whole thing protected by ditches and timber palisad When time and money allowed the timber defences were replaced wit strong stone walls. The castle above is the motte and bailey at York.

1064 Harold Godwinson swears an oath of allegiance to William of Normandy. **1066** Edward the Confessor	dies and is succeeded by Harold Godwinson. **1066** Duke William of Normandy invades	England to claim throne. **1066** Battle of Hastings - William of Normandy defeats Harold and becomes king as William I.	**1068/9** Harrying of the North. **1070** Lanfranc appointed	Archbishop of Canterbu **1070** Canterbury Cathedra destroyed by fire. Lanfranc begins buildin

🏠 ARCHITECTURE   📖 ARTS & LITERATURE   ↪ EXPLORATION   ⚔ FAMOUS BATTLE

CORONATION

Following his victory at Hastings, on 14th October 1066, William then marched on London, putting down local opposition as he went. He was crowned on Christmas Day the same year in Westminster Abbey.

ROYAL FORTRESS

The Tower of London was begun in 1078 when William ordered its construction, in one. It soon became the principal royal residence and prison and has been added to in every century since then. The original mound was known (at least from the 6th century) as the 'White Mount', from where the 'White Tower' takes its name and not, as is popularly supposed, from being painted white in the Middle Ages, as many castles were.

SAXON REBELLION

Hereward the Wake led a Saxon rebellion against the Normans from his secret hideaway in the marshes surrounding the Isle of Ely, in Cambridgeshire. William defeated the rebels in 1071.

BISHOP ODO

Odo was William I's half-brother and came across with the Conqueror in 1066. He was created Earl of Kent and later Bishop of Bayeux, although he was always more interested in acquiring land and power than in affairs of the church. He led an unsuccessful rebellion against William and was banished from England in 1082.

WILLIAM I
BORN 1027 • ACCEDED 1066 • DIED 1087

*W*illiam was the illegitimate son of Robert, Duke of Normandy, who inherited that title at the age of eight. He had been promised the English throne in 1051 by Edward the Confessor, whose mother was of Norman descent. When Edward later went back on his word and promised succession to his brother-in-law Harold Godwinson, William decided to take the throne by force. After the battle William subdued the Saxons by confiscating their land and giving it to his Norman supporters. He was a fair if sometimes brutal ruler and died after falling from his horse during a military campaign in France.

to a much larger plan.	**1072**	*Tower of London,*	*enclosed for royal hunting.*	*of all land holdings,*
1071	*William I invades Scotland*	*one of the earliest*	**1080**	*is begun.*
Hereward the Wake	*and wins homage from*	*stone castles built*	*William refuses to pay*	**1087**
(leader of Saxon revolt	*Malcolm III.*	*in England.*	*homage to the pope.*	*William I dies in a horse*
against Normans)	**1077/8**	**1079**	**1085**	*riding accident during*
is defeated.	*Work begins on the*	*New Forest in Hampshire*	*Domesday Book, a survey*	*siege of Nantes.*

🜍 GOVERNMENT   ⚗ HEALTH & MEDICINE   ⚖ JUSTICE   ✝ RELIGION   🗲 SCIENCE

WILLIAM II

BORN 1056(?) • ACCEDED 1087 • DIED 1100

When William I died his lands were divided amongst his two eldest sons, Robert, who inherited Normandy, and William, who became king of England. Although, as invaders, none of the Norman kings were popular with the Saxons, William I had at least been a strong and just ruler. His son William, known as 'Rufus' because of the reddish colour of his hair and complexion, was more ruthless and less judicial than his father. He never married and on his death the throne passed to his younger brother, Henry.

A CORRUPT BULLY

William held a lascivious court and openly extracted money from the church, but it was the actions of his mercenary soldiers that attracted most criticism. Villagers were said to desert their homes when the king's entourage approached rather than submit to their brutality.

ANSELM

When Lanfranc, the Archbishop of Canterbury, died the position fell vacant for four years. William installed Anselm, a Benedictine monk from France, in 1093 but he rowed with the king over high taxation and was forced into exile in 1097. Three years later Henry I recalled him to power.

A HUNTING ACCIDENT?

William was killed, supposedly, in a hunting accident in the New Forest on 2nd August 1100. A chance arrow, fired by Walter Tyrell, glanced off a tree and struck the king, although it has been suggested his brother Henry, as heir to the throne, may have given orders for his assassination. The 'Rufus Stone' marks the spot in the forest today.

1087	**1088**	to the throne.	from Scotland and	**1093**
William I's second eldest	William defeats	**1090**	annexed to England.	Malcolm III of
son becomes William II	rebellion led by his	William leads unsuccessful	**1093**	Scotland invades
of England, his eldest son	uncle, Bishop Odo in	invasion of Normandy	Anselm becomes	England and
Robert succeeds as	Normandy in support	**1092**	Archbishop	is killed
Duke of Normandy.	of Robert's claim	Cumberland captured	of Canterbury.	in the process.

🏛 ARCHITECTURE   📖 ARTS & LITERATURE   EXPLORATION   💧 FAMOUS BATTLE

WESTMINSTER HALL

William ordered the construction of Westminster Hall in 1097 on the site of an earlier palace. The great hammerbeam roof was added in the 1390s. It remained the principal royal residence until Henry VIII's reign, but most of the buildings burned down in 1834. The Houses of Parliament now occupy much of the site.

INVASION BY SCOTLAND

Malcolm III of Scotland invaded England on five separate occasions in an attempt to annex the counties of Northumberland, Cumberland and Westmorland to Scotland. The last time was in 1093 when he was killed by William II at the Battle of Alnwick.

THE BARONS' REVOLT

William's brother Robert laid claim to the English throne and led a baronial revolt against him, supported by their uncle, Bishop Odo. William crushed the revolt in 1088 and another, in Northumberland, in 1095.

🏛 DURHAM CATHEDRAL

The present cathedral (above) was begun in 1093 and remains one of the finest Norman buildings in the country. It contains the body of St. Cuthbert, a seventh century Celtic monk, whose tomb was a centre of pilgrimage throughout the Middle Ages.

THE ROYAL SPORT

The Norman kings enjoyed hunting, almost to the point of obsession, and gave over large tracts of land for the pursuit. Stags were popular quarry, as were wolves and wild boar, which were not yet extinct in England.

1095 William puts down a baronial revolt in Northumbria.	*a 'holy war' to recover the Holy Lands from the Muslims.*	*Jerusalem, but success is short lived.*	**1097** *William begins construction of Westminster Hall.*	*against Norman rule put down.*
1095 *Pope Urban II calls*	**1096/7** *First crusade to the Holy Lands regains*	**1097** *Anselm exiled to Rome and all his estates forfeited to crown.*	**1098** *Welsh rebellion*	**1100** *William II is killed in a hunting accident in the New Forest.*

🏛 GOVERNMENT   ⚕ HEALTH & MEDICINE   ⚖ JUSTICE   ✝ RELIGION   ✒ SCIENCE

HENRY I

BORN 1068 • ACCEDED 1100 • DIED 1135

UNFAITHFUL HUSBAND

Henry married Edith, the daughter of Malcolm III, king of Scotland, and so united the two countries. She used the name Matilda and they remained married for 18 years. Henry had several mistresses who bore him no less than 22 illegitimate children.

'LION OF JUSTICE'

Henry was a shrewd man who knew he had to placate the Saxon population to strengthen his position. On succeeding to the throne he promised good governance and introduced several legal reforms, including an improved judiciary.

ROCHESTER CASTLE

Rochester Castle was first built in 1086 by Bishop Gundulph and guarded an important crossing of the main London to Dover road over the River Medway, in Kent. The magnificent keep was added in 1127, built by royal charter issued by Henry. It is the tallest keep in Europe and remains one of the most original Norman buildings still standing.

*T*he circumstances of William II's death had always been regarded with suspicion, but because he was so disliked by lord and peasant alike little attempt was made to solve the mystery and his death was never avenged. Chief among the suspects was Henry, William I's youngest son, who was in the vicinity at the time and on hearing news of his brother's death seized the royal treasure at Winchester and rode straight to London to declare himself king.

CLAIM TO THE THRONE

The rightful heir to the English throne on William II's death was his son Robert, already Duke of Normandy. Henry, Robert's younger brother, seized the crown and proclaimed himself king three days later. On hearing the news Robert invaded England to claim the throne. After several attempts he eventually failed and was imprisoned by Henry , who then seized his lands in Normandy.

1100 William's brother becomes king as Henry I. **1100** Henry marries	*daughter of Malcolm III, King of Scotland.* **1100** *Charter of Liberties issued.*	**1101** *Robert of Normandy invades England but is repulsed by Henry.* **1101** *Court of the*	*Exchequer is founded.* **1106** *War breaks out between Henry and Robert again.* *Robert defeated and held prisoner. Henry seizes*	*Robert's lands in Normandy.* **1110** *Archbishop Anselm die* **1110** *Pipe Rolls introduced.*

🏛 ARCHITECTURE   📖 ARTS & LITERATURE   ⚑ EXPLORATION   💣 FAMOUS BATTLE

THE WHITE SHIP

The 'White Ship', reputedly the finest vessel of its day, ran aground and sank in the Channel in November 1120, while returning from Normandy. Henry's only legitimate son and heir, William, drowned in the accident caused, it is believed, by a drunken crew. His death left the crown without a male heir, resulting in years of civil war between King Stephen and Henry's daughter the Empress Matilda.

🥣 LEPER HOSPITAL

St. Bartholomew's Hospital, in London, was founded in 1123 and is reputed to be the oldest hospital in England. Early medieval hospitals were mostly run by the church and did not provide health care in the modern sense, but simply provided 'hospitality' in the form of food and lodging for the chronically sick, usually lepers, who could not look after themselves.

⚖ CHARTER OF LIBERTIES

Immediately he succeeded to the throne Henry issued a Charter of Liberties promising the people of England that he would govern well and fairly, treating Saxon and Norman equally.

⚖ PIPE ROLLS

Henry made sheriffs and other royal officials accountable by introducing the Pipe Rolls, which detailed all official expenditure. They remained in use until 1834.

HEIR TO THE THRONE

The year after the 'White Ship' tragedy Henry married again, to Adela of Louvain, in the hope of producing another son, but the marriage was fruitless. Instead, Henry had to try and persuade his barons to accept his daughter Matilda as his heir.

UNTIMELY DEATH

Henry had long feared an assassination attempt and slept with his sword by his side. He died, it is believed from food poisoning, after eating infected lampreys (a sea-food) at Rouen, in France.

THE GREAT SEAL

This picture shows the great royal seal of Henry I. All of the medieval kings had their own, individual seal, usually depicting the monarch himself. Made of embossed metal it was used to seal all official letters and writs by pressing it firmly into hot wax. Only authorised people could break the seal and read the contents of the document.

1118 Henry's wife Matilda, dies. **1120** Henry's son and heir William dies in 'White	Ship' tragedy. **1121** Henry marries Adela of Louvain. **1123** St. Bartholomew's	Hospital founded in London. **1126** Henry persuades barons to accept Matilda, his daughter as queen,	on his death. **1135** Henry I dies of food poisoning at Rouen, in France.

🏛 GOVERNMENT   🥣 HEALTH & MEDICINE   ⚖ JUSTICE   ✝ RELIGION   📖 SCIENCE

STEPHEN
BORN 1096 • ACCEDED 1135 • DIED 1154

& MATILDA
BORN 1102 • ACCEDED 1141 • DEPOSED 1141 • DIED 1167

Stephen had sworn his allegiance to Matilda as heir to the throne, along with most other barons, but when Henry I died he usurped the throne and had himself crowned king. Almost the entire duration of his reign was spent in civil war as the barons divided their allegiance between him and Matilda. Although a good-natured and courteous man, he was also weak. A state of anarchy developed in which the barons plundered the country at will while, it was said, 'Christ and His saints slept'.

SIEGE OF OXFORD

The turning point in the civil war came in 1142 when Stephen besieged Matilda in Oxford Castle. One night, after three months of stalemate, Matilda escaped in a white robe over the frozen river Isis. Shortly afterwards the garrison was starved into submission.

MATILDA FLEES

In 1145 Stephen won a resounding victory over Matilda at the Battle of Faringdon. Three years later she gave up the fight and left England for France.

RIVAL CLAIMANTS

When Henry I's only legitimate son, William, died in 1120 his daughter Matilda became heir to the throne. Henry spent the last years of his reign persuading the barons to swear allegiance to her. However, Henry's nephew Stephen, by his sister Adela, also claimed the throne on the grounds that as William I's eldest surviving grandson he was the rightful heir.

1135
Henry's nephew, Stephen, usurps the throne from Matilda, Henry's daughter.

1136
Civil war breaks out between barons who support either Stephen or Matilda.

1138
David I of Scotland invades England in support of his niece, Matilda.

1138
David I defeated by Stephen

at Battle of the Standard.
1139
Matilda returns to England from France to claim throne.

1141
Stephen captured at

Lincoln, and is then imprisoned at Bristol Castle. Matilda rules for just 6 months, but is not crowned.

🏛 ARCHITECTURE   📖 ARTS & LITERATURE   ⚑ EXPLORATION   ☄ FAMOUS BATTLE

ARUNDEL CASTLE

..rundel Castle, in Sussex, was begun in the late 11th century and was granted by Henry I to the Albini family. In 1139 William de Albini, who supported Matilda in the civil war, gave shelter to her. When Stephen arrived at the castle with his army to besiege it, Matilda fled to the West Country.

FAVERSHAM ABBEY

Stephen and his wife, also named Matilda, were buried at Faversham Abbey, in Kent, which he had founded some years earlier. The abbey was almost totally destroyed at the Dissolution and the royal tombs thrown into the nearby creek. A plaque in the church of St. Mary of Charity states that their bones were transferred there.

THE KING HELD PRISONER

In 1141 Matilda's supporters defeated Stephen at the Battle of Lincoln. He was taken prisoner and held at Bristol Castle, but was afterwards exchanged for Robert, Earl of Gloucester, Matilda's half-brother. During Stephen's confinement Matilda briefly declared herself queen for six months. ..on entering London Matilda upset the people of the city with her arrogance. ..ey forced her to leave, preventing her from formally claiming the throne.

⬥ BATTLE OF THE STANDARD

Matilda's uncle, David I of Scotland, lent his support to her cause by invading the north of England in 1138, but he was defeated by Stephen's army at the Battle of the Standard at Northallerton, in Yorkshire.

▣ TREATY OF WESTMINSTER

In 1153 Henry of Anjou, Matilda's son, took up the claim for the English throne where his mother had left off. Henry quickly gathered support and at the Treaty of Westminster it was agreed that Stephen should remain king until his death, but then the throne should pass to Henry and not to Stephen's heirs, bringing 19 years of civil war to an end.

MATILDA

Matilda was born in 1102 to Henry I and Edith of Scotland, also known as Matilda. She was arrogant, had a fiery temper and a quite objectionable nature that caused many of her allies to desert her. In 1129 she married Geoffrey Plantagenet, Count of Anjou. Their son ruled England as Henry II, so beginning a new royal dynasty, the Plantagenets.

1142 Matilda escapes from the siege of Oxford.	Battle of Farringdon. **1148** Matilda concedes defeat and flees England for Anjou.	succeeds his father Geoffrey, as Count of Anjou. **1153** Henry re-opens civil	**1153** Treaty of Westminster, Stephen agrees to pass throne to Henry	**1154** Stephen dies and the throne passes to Matilda's son, Henry
1145 Stephen defeats Matilda at the	**1151** Matilda's son, Henry,	war with Stephen.	Plantagenet on his death and not to his son William.	Plantagenet, who becomes king as Henry II.

🗓 GOVERNMENT 🥄 HEALTH & MEDICINE ⚖ JUSTICE ✝ RELIGION ▯ SCIENCE

HENRY II

BORN 1133 • ACCEDED 1154 • DIED 1189

INVASION OF IRELAND

In 1155 Pope Adrian IV (left) gave sanction to Henry to invade Ireland and bring its church under papal control. In 1166 Henry sent an army to Ireland, led by Richard de Clare, Earl of Pembroke, following an appeal by one of the Irish kings, Dermot MacMurrough, king of Leinster, to help him crush opposition by the other Irish chieftains. Five years later Henry invaded Ireland himself and soon earned homage from all the Irish kings and proclaimed himself Lord of Ireland. Later that year, at the Council of Cashel, Henry forced the Irish church to submit to papal authority.

LICENCE TO CRENELLATE

During the civil wars of Stephen's reign a state of anarchy existed and many barons erected castles unlawfully. One of Henry's first acts was to destroy all unlicensed, or adulterine castles and replace them with royal strongholds. Any baron who wanted to fortify his house had to seek a 'licence to crenellate' from the king.

DOVER CASTLE

Dover Castle, at the nearest point between England and France, stands high on the cliffs overlooking the town and is one of our finest medieval castles. A great favourite of Henry's, he expended a great deal of money on its construction. The magnificent keep he built is one of the largest and most complex such structures ever built. It is surrounded by two tiers of concentric curtain walls, containing a fine array of towers and gatehouses.

*f*ollowing the turmoil of Stephen's reign, England needed a strong king to re-unite a divided nation. It found him in Henry I the son of Matilda and Geoffrey Plantagenet. He came to the throne at just 21, a strong, robust and well-educated man. Despite a fiery temper, he wa a just man who ruled well and introduced many legal and church reforms.

THOMAS BECKET

Thomas Becket was born of humble parents in 1118. In about 1144 he entered service to Theobald, Archbishop of Canterbury. A well-educated man, Theobald recommended him to Henry II, who in 115 appointed him Chancellor. Becket and Henry quickly became friend and he actively supported many of the king's reforms. When Henry made him archbishop in 1162 he expected Becket to continue with his support, but Becket took his new position seriously and oppose Henry's church reforms. They quarrelled and Becket was forced into exile in France between 1164-70.

THE MURDER OF BECKET

Threatened with excommunication, Henry allowed Becket to return to England in 1170, but the two soon quarrelled again. The king is said to have exclaimed aloud: 'Will no-one rid me of this turbulent priest?' Whereupon four of his knights set out for Canterbury and murdered Becket in his own cathedral on 29th December 1170. Three years later Becket was canonised.

🏛 ARCHITECTURE   📖 ARTS & LITERATURE   🏴 EXPLORATION   💣 FAMOUS BATTLE

OXFORD UNIVERSITY FOUNDED

In 1168 English scholars, who had been studying at Paris, were expelled. They returned to England, settling at Oxford, which was already acquiring a name for itself as a centre of learning, and founded a university there. In 1264 the first college, Merton, was founded. Several more quickly followed, establishing Oxford as the foremost university in Europe.

✝ CONSTITUTIONS OF CLARENDON

In January 1164 Henry issued the 'Constitutions of Clarendon', a set of 16 articles attempting to curb the power of the church in England, which had grown considerably during the anarchy of Stephen's reign. Principal among them was Henry's claim that clerics who broke the law should be punished by secular courts and not have their punishments decided by the church, which formed the root of the quarrel with Becket.

⚖ ASSIZE OF CLARENDON

Clarendon Palace was one of Henry's favourite royal residences and he issued many writs from there, including the 'Assize of Clarendon', which introduced the idea of trial by jury for the first time. (Assizes were the periodic sessions by Westminster judges in county courts.)

REBELLIOUS FAMILY

In 1152 Henry married Eleanor of Aquitaine, but his family life was far from happy. Between 1173-4 his sons Henry, Geoffrey, Richard and John rebelled against him, encouraged by Eleanor. He put down the rebellion and kept Eleanor a virtual prisoner for the last 15 years of his reign.

THE KING'S PENANCE

Whether he was directly responsible or not for Becket's murder, Henry was certainly implicated and accepted a public penance for his martyrdom, which included flagellation by the monks of Christ Church, Canterbury. Becket's tomb at Canterbury became the most popular place of pilgrimage in England until Henry VIII dissolved the monasteries in 1536-40.

---

troduces trial by jury.
1166
*irst invasion force by
igland sent to Ireland
i response to request
one of the Irish kings,*

Dermot McMurrough.
1168
*English scholars
expelled from Paris,
leads to foundation of
Oxford University.*

1170
*Becket is murdered at
Canterbury Cathedral.*
1171
*Henry II invades
Ireland receives homage of*

*Irish kings and is accepted
as Lord of Ireland.*
1171
*Council of Cashel makes
Irish church acknowledge
authority of Rome.*

1173
*Becket is canonised.
Pilgrims begin visiting
shrine at Canterbury.*
1189
Henry dies in Anjou.

15

📜 GOVERNMENT　　🥣 HEALTH & MEDICINE　　⚖ JUSTICE　　✝ RELIGION　　📖 SCIENCE

RICHARD COEUR DE LION

Richard is usually depicted as a brave, warrior king, earning him the nickname 'Lionheart'. Although undoubtedly a competent soldier, he was also a very cruel man. After the fall of Acre he ordered 2,700 captured Muslims to be executed.

THE CRUSADES

The Crusades were a series of wars (nine in all) waged from 1095 to liberate the Holy Land from Islamic rule. Though all of the crusades failed in their objective, there was no shortage of volunteers, who might win remission for their sins by defeating the heathens.

A KING'S RANSOM

On his return from Palestine Richard was captured by Leopold, of Austria, and imprisoned by Henry VI, Emperor of Germany. A huge ransom was demanded for his safe return, which was raised in England, mostly through heavy taxation.

RICHARD I

BORN 1157 • ACCEDED 1189 • DIED 1199

ichard I was born on 8th September 1157 at Beaumor Palace in Oxford. The third and eldest surviving son of Henry II and Eleanor of Aquitaine, he succeeded to the throne in 1189. Richard spent barely seven months of his 10 year reign in this country, and three of those were in the first year of his accession. His queen, Berengaria of Navarre, never set foot in England. A powerfully-built man, he was also musical and well-educated, though he spoke little English. He used England merely as a source of revenue to finance his wars abroad.

SALADIN

Saladin (Salah-ad-Din, 1138-93) was a Turkish leader of Kurdish descent who defeated the Fatimid dynasty in Egypt and declared himself Sultan. In 1187 he seized Jerusalem, which prompted the Third Crusade, when the combined forces of Western Christendom were sent against him. Although often depicted as a cruel man, he was in fact a very learned patron of the arts and sciences, much respected for his generosity and chivalry.

1189 Henry's eldest son becomes king as Richard I. **1189** Richard embarks upon	the Third Crusade to the Holy Land with Philip of France. **1189** William Longchamp appointed Chancellor to	govern England in Richard's absence. **1189** Scotland gains independence (surrendered to Henry II in 1173)	from Richard in return for cash payment to help finance his crusades to Holy Lands. **1191** Longchamp falls	from power and Prince John assumes government of the country during Richard's absence.

 ARCHITECTURE ARTS & LITERATURE 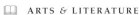 EXPLORATION  FAMOUS BATTLE

CHÂTEAU GAILLARD

Richard I supervised the building of Château Gaillard, in Normandy, overlooking the Seine at Les Andelys. Built in just two years (1196-98) it incorporated many sophisticated innovations, including concentric walls, rock-cut ditches and an elliptical citadel at the centre. It stood at the boundary between Richard's duchy in Normandy and the French king's lands. Once considered impregnable, it fell to Philip II of France in 1204.

A ROYAL PARDON

Following his return from captivity in 1194, Richard stayed in England only a few months before departing to protect his dominions in France. He was shot by a crossbow-man during the siege of Chalus-Chabrol. The wound turned gangrenous, but he forgave the bowman on his deathbed on 6th April 1199. He was buried at Fontevrault Abbey and was the last English monarch to be buried in France.

THE CRUSADES

The Third Crusade, led by Richard I, was the most successful. The crusaders suffered terribly in the heat, and from disease, especially dysentery. Richard took the city of Acre and reached an agreement with Saladin to allow Christians free passage to Jerusalem, but the holy city remained in Muslim hands until 1917.

ROBIN HOOD

In the popular legend of Robin Hood, a disinherited Saxon nobleman led a band of outlaws against the tyranny of John, Richard,s brother (who ruled England in Richard's absence) robbing the rich to give to the oppressed poor. While his existence cannot be proved with any certainty, stories of his exploits were circulating as early as 1262.

1191
Richard captures city of Acre in the Holy Land and defeats Saladin at Arsouf.

1192
Richard makes agreement with Saladin to allow Christians to enter Jerusalem without fear of recriminations.

1192
Richard is captured on his return from Palestine by Duke of Austria who hands him over to Henry VI, Emperor of Germany.

Richard is held to ransom.
1194
Ransom paid and Richard is released.
1194
Richard returns to

England but leaves soon after to defend his lands in France.
1199
Richard is killed at Chalus, in France.

GOVERNMENT   HEALTH & MEDICINE   JUSTICE   RELIGION   SCIENCE

JOHN

BORN 1166 • ACCEDED 1199 • DIED 1216

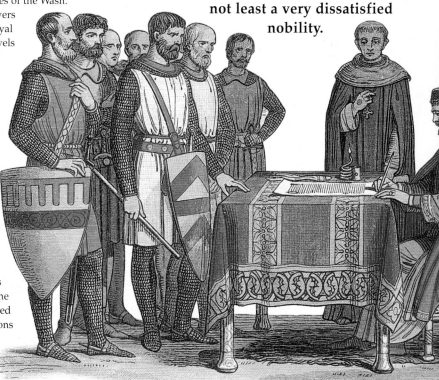

LOSS OF THE CROWN JEWELS

Shortly before his death John's entourage met with an accident in the treacherous marshes of the Wash. Several of his followers drowned and the royal chest, containing jewels and a great deal of money, was lost.

ohn's reign is overshadowed by one or tw major events of the period, which belie th realities. He was an able administrator an a much better king than history has portrayed hir In truth, although he was implicated in a plot to usurp the crown from his brother, many of the problems he faced were in fact caused by Richard who had neglected England. The cost of the Third Crusade and Richard's ransom had to be met through high taxation. John inherited a near bankrupt country with many inherent problems, not least a very dissatisfied nobility.

THE BARONS REBEL

The conflict between John and his barons had been building up over many years. High taxation, disputes with the church, the loss of the French domains and tampering with the legal system culminated in civil war, the barons claiming that John had abused his royal powers.

1199		1209	king of England.	to Holy Land.
Richard's brother,	France to Philip II.	John is excommunicated	1212	Most died or were
John, becomes king.	1208	by the pope.	Children's Crusade, -ill-	sold into slavery.
1204	Pope Innocent III issues	1212	fated crusade by	1213
John loses most	an Interdict against	Pope declares John is	30,000 children from	John gives in to
of his lands in	England, banning	no longer the rightful	France and Germany	pope's demands.
	most church services.			

 ARCHITECTURE   ARTS & LITERATURE   EXPLORATION   FAMOUS BATTLE

PRINCE OF PLEASURE

John was well-educated and quite fastidious. He liked to dress in fine clothes and take frequent baths. He enjoyed entertaining at court and had a passion for hunting.

'LACKLAND'

Although England accepted John as king, the barons in France regarded Arthur, John's nephew by his dead elder brother Geoffrey, to be the rightful heir to the Plantagenet empire. War broke out with France, which went disastrously for John. By 1204 he had lost virtually all his French lands, earning him the title 'John Lackland'.

EXCOMMUNICATION

John frequently quarrelled with the church, particularly over the pope's choice of Stephen Langton as Archbishop of Canterbury. He seized much of the church's property in England, an act for which he was excommunicated in 1209.

✟ INTERDICT

In 1208 John incurred the wrath of the pope, Innocent III, who responded by issuing an Interdict against England. All church services were banned, with the exception of baptisms and funerals.

💣✳ SIEGE OF ROCHESTER CASTLE

In October 1215 rebellious barons seized the royal castle at Rochester, in Kent. John, seldom given due credit for his military prowess, personally supervised siege operations to retake it. His miners and sappers succeeded in bringing down the south-east corner of the keep, a remarkable achievement. The garrison capitulated after just six weeks.

SUSPICIOUS DEATH

Following the tragedy of the Wash, John made his way to Newark Castle, in Nottinghamshire, one of the king's favourite residences. He is supposed to have caught a fever and died a few days later. The circumstances of his death were suspicious, but never investigated, because with his passing the civil war between the barons ended.

MAGNA CARTA

The barons turned to Stephen Langton, Archbishop of Canterbury, who helped them draw up the Great Charter. The original draft signed by John on 15th June 1215 contained 63 clauses outlining the rights and responsibilities of the crown and the nobles. The king was no longer allowed to govern at will, but only within the confines of the charter. Many of the clauses were specific to the barons and the rights of the church and had little effect on the lives of ordinary people, but it is now regarded as a milestone in our constitutional history. Several versions of the charter, with amendments, were drawn up, the last one signed by Henry III in 1225.

1214 French defeat John at Battle of Bouvines.	discuss terms of Magna Carta.	the Magna Carta at Runneymede.	**1216** John loses his personal possessions in the Wash.	to help in civil war with John.
1214 English barons meet at Bury St. Edmunds to	**1215** John reluctantly agrees to barons' demands and signs	**1215** Pope allows John to ignore Magna Carta; civil war ensues.	**1216** Barons invite French Prince, Louis,	**1216** John dies at Newark castle (foul-play is suspected).

⚖ GOVERNMENT 🥄 HEALTH & MEDICINE ⚖️ JUSTICE ✟ RELIGION 🔬 SCIENCE

HENRY III

BORN 1207 • ACCEDED 1216 • DIED 1272

enry was only nine years old when his father, John, died in 1216. John, perhaps anticipating his demise, had already made provisions for a regent to rule during Henry's minority. After 1227 Henry took control of the government, but years of misrule eventually led to civil war again, this time resulting in the formation of a parliament. Despite these problems, Henry's was a long reign, marked by many advancements in architecture and the arts.

HENRY'S RELATIONSHIP WITH HIS BARONS

The growth of Parliament occurred during Henry III's reign, largely because of his embittered relationship with his barons, inherited from his father, King John. The situation was made worse after his marriage to Eleanor of Provence in 1236 when he gave several French noblemen influential positions of power at court.

THE 'DAUPHIN' OF FRANCE

During the civil war of John's reign the rebel barons had invited the French prince, Louis, to take the throne of England. Following John's death, many barons withdrew their support in favour of Henry. Louis was finally defeated at Lincoln in 1217 and returned to France.

SIMON DE MONTFORT

Known as the 'father of English Parliament', Simon de Montfort was leader of the rebel barons in the ongoing civil war with the king. Although parliaments, or councils, had been known since Saxon times, de Montfort was determined to make government more accountable and open to all classes, and not reliant on the whims of the ruling monarch. He defeated Henry at Lewes in 1264 and called the first open English Parliament the following year.

THE REGENCY

Between 1216-27 England was ruled by two regents, William the Marshal, Earl of Pembroke, and Hubert de Burgh, two very capable administrators. William died in 1219 and when Henry took control in 1227 he retained Hubert de Burgh as his adviser.

1216	1217	1219	down attempt by Louis VIII	1233/4
Henry III becomes king at just nine years old.	Treaty of Lambeth creates peace between England and France	William the Marshal dies. Hubert de Burgh rules alone.	of France to seize English throne.	Rebellion against the ki led by Richard Marsha
1217	and between the king	**1222**	**1227**	Earl of Pembroke defeat
A French attempt to seize the English throne fails.	and his barons.	Hubert de Burgh puts	Henry assumes control of government.	**1238** Simon de Montfort

 ARCHITECTURE   ARTS & LITERATURE   EXPLORATION    FAMOUS BATTLE

AGE OF LEARNING

Although not the ablest of political leaders, Henry was a great patron of the arts. During his reign the universities of Oxford and Cambridge both flourished.

KENILWORTH CASTLE

Kenilworth Castle, in Warwickshire, was first built about 1120 by Geoffrey de Clinton and was later granted to Simon de Montfort. He used it as his base during the civil war with Henry III. By Tudor times the castle had assumed palatial proportions and was one of the finest residences in the country. The castle afterwards passed to the Earls of Leicester. Elizabeth I stayed there with Lord Dudley for 19 days during one of her royal progresses.

📜 PROVISIONS OF OXFORD

At a meeting of parliament in Oxford in 1258 the rebel barons forced Henry to sign a series of documents which effectively limited absolute royal power. Henry rebuked the 'provisions' in 1261 and ignored them altogether after de Montfort's death in 1265.

📜 THE FIRST ENGLISH PARLIAMENT

Although the idea of a parliament, where the views of people from different factions could be heard, had been in existence for several centuries, it carried few constitutional rights. Parliament usually consisted of a handful of the king's trusted allies and acted mostly in an advisory capacity. The parliament called by Simon de Montfort in 1265 is regarded as a milestone in constitutional history because, for the first time, it took the views of all social groups, except peasants, into account.

💣 BATTLE OF EVESHAM

Some of the rebel barons decided to leave Simon de Montfort to take the king's side in the civil war. Henry's son, Edward, defeated de Montfort at the Battle of Evesham in 1265. Although the seeds of parliamentary government had been sown, Henry resumed control of the country for the remainder of his reign.

marries Henry's sister, Eleanor.	**1258** Provisions of Oxford, limits royal power.	of Oxford, which leads to further baronial revolt.	**1265** Simon de Montfort summons the first	killed at the Battle of Evesham.
1258 Simon de Montfort leads revolt against Henry's misgovernment.	**1261** Henry refuses to acknowledge the Provisions	**1264** Baron's war breaks out, Henry defeated by de Montfort.	English Parliament. **1265** Simon de Montfort	**1272** Henry III dies at Westminster.

📜 GOVERNMENT   ⚕ HEALTH & MEDICINE   ⚖ JUSTICE   ✝ RELIGION   📖 SCIENCE

📜 MODEL PARLIAMENT

Following on from the political reforms of his father's reign, Edward is credited with calling the first democratically elected parliament (at least partially) known as the 'Model Parliament', which comprised lords, clergy, knights and elected representatives from the shires and towns.

⚖️ STATUTE OF WINCHESTER

The first Justices of the Peace were introduced as a result of the 'Statute of Winchester' in 1285, along with controls against highway robbery and the right for local communities to police themselves against violent attacks.

💣 BATTLE OF STIRLING BRIDGE

The Scots rose against Edward in 1297 under the leadership of William Wallace, who defeated Edward at the Battle of Stirling Bridge.

💣 BATTLE OF FALKIRK

Edward turned the tables on Wallace in 1298 when he defeated him at the Battle of Falkirk. Wallace continued to lead Scottish resistance against the English until his arrest and execution in 1305, after which Robert Bruce led the revolt against Edward.

PRINCE LLWELYN

The last independent Prince of Wales, Llwelyn Yr Ail, refused to acknowledge Edward as overlord of Wales and led several rebellions against him from his Snowdonia stronghold. He was overcome and killed at Builth in 1282. Two years later all of Wales finally subjected to Edward.

CAERNARFON CASTLE

Caernarfon Castle was begun in 1282 and from the start was meant to impress newly conquered Welsh as his new capital. The high walls, incorporating seven massive towers and gatehouses, are constructed of coloured bands of masonry purposely mimicking the walls of Constantinople. The internal lodgings were never completed and it remains virtually intact today, one of the finest medieval castles ever built.

CONQUEST OF WALES

Edward launched his conquest of Wales in 1277. Much of southern and mid-Wales quickly submitted to his rule, but the people of north Wales held out from their mountain retreats in Snowdonia until 1284. Edward built a ring of mighty castles and established walled towns with English settlements to subjugate them. In 1301 he declared his son, Edward, to be the Prince of Wales, a title still held by the ruling monarch's eldest son.

1272 Edward I becomes king whilst on Crusade to the Holy Land. **1274** Edward I returns to England and is crowned king.	**1277** Edward invades North Wales in an attempt to force Prince Llewelyn to pay homage. **1279** Statute of Mortmain issued	to stop land being given to the church to avoid taxes. **1282** Edward invades North Wales again and defeats Prince Llewelyn.	**1284** Statute of Rhuddlan ends Welsh independence. **1285** Statute of Winchester controls highway robbery and	introduces Justices of the Pe **1290** Edward expels Jews from England. **1292** Edward elects John Balliol

🏛 ARCHITECTURE 📖 ARTS & LITERATURE ✒ EXPLORATION 💣 FAMOUS BATTLE

'LONGSHANKS'

Edward was over 6 ft. tall, when the average height was about 5 ft. 4 ins., earning him the title 'longshanks'. An athletic, robust man, with jet black hair, he was considered handsome, though he is believed to have had a slight speech impediment.

ELEANOR OF CASTILE

Edward married Eleanor of Castile in 1254 and together they had 16 children. He was devoted to her and was heartbroken when she died. When her body was carried from Nottinghamshire to Westminster he had a memorial cross erected at each of the 12 resting places, including Charing Cross, in London.

'HAMMER OF THE SCOTS'

Although Edward earned the nickname 'Hammer of the Scots', he never fully conquered Scotland. In 1292 he was asked to mediate in choosing the Scottish heir and chose John Balliol, a weak man who paid homage to Edward. When Balliol rebelled against him Edward invaded Scotland and declared himself king. The Scots refused to accept him and Edward died in 1307 on his third attempt to conquer Scotland.

JEWS EXPELLED

In 1290 Edward instigated the first banishment of the Jews, more on political and financial grounds than as religious persecution. He seized all their property and any debts still owed to them.

EDWARD I

BORN 1239 • ACCEDED 1272 • DIED 1307

Edward was away on the 8th Crusade to the Holy Land, with his uncle Louis IX of France, when he heard of his father's death. Louis died of plague in 1270 but Edward continued to Acre only to find the allied leaders in disarray. The crusade failed and Edward returned home to be crowned king, in August 1274. He was a formidable soldier who spent much of his reign trying to unite England, Scotland and Wales into one kingdom, with partial success. He was also a very able and just ruler, responsible for many political and social reforms.

STONE OF SCONE

The kings of Scotland had for centuries been crowned at Scone Abbey. The ceremonial coronation stone (a large, rectangular boulder believed to date from prehistoric times) was seized by Edward I in 1296 when he declared himself king of Scotland. It was taken to Westminster Abbey and placed beneath the coronation throne, where it stayed until 1996, when it was returned to Scotland, not to Scone, which is now ruinous, but to Edinburgh Castle.

23

GOVERNMENT   HEALTH & MEDICINE   JUSTICE   RELIGION   SCIENCE

EDWARD II

BORN 1284 • ACCEDED 1307 • DEPOSED 1307 • DIED 1327

Edward II was the fourth, but eldest surviving son of Edward I. His reign is best remembered for its lack of military campaigning, unlike his father's, and also for the gruesome circumstances surrounding his death. Although often dismissed as an inept administrator, England actually prospered during his rule, due in no small part to low taxation; his father had raised taxes considerably to pay for his wars in Wales and Scotland.

THE KING IS MURDERED

Following his dispossession, Edward was held prisoner in Kenilworth Castle, where he formally abdicated the throne. He was then imprisoned at Berkeley Castle, Gloucestershire, for six months. On the instructions of Isabella, Edward was murdered by the insertion of a red-hot poker into his rectum - a punishment normally reserved for homosexuals. The story goes that the king's screams could be heard outside the castle.

PIERS GAVESTON

Edward had little interest in government and entrusted much of the day-to-day work to a few ill-chosen but trusted advisers. One of these, Piers Gaveston, angered the barons because of his mismanagement. In 1312 he was captured and murdered by the king's enemies.

ISABELLA OF FRANCE

Edward married Isabella of France in 1308 and she bore him four children, but it was a loveless marriage. She openly had an affair with her lover, Roger Mortimer, and in 1326 they led a rebellion against the king, forcing his deposition in favour of his son.

1307
Edward, Prince of Wales accedes to the throne as Edward II.
1308
King's favourite, Piers Gaveston,

exiled for mismanagement of state affairs.
1309
Gaveston returns from exile.
1310
Edward's cousin Thomas,

 ARCHITECTURE   ARTS & LITERATURE   EXPLORATION   FAMOUS BATTLE

BATTLE OF BANNOCKBURN

Robert Bruce finally crushed the English at the Battle of Bannockburn in 1314, near Stirling Castle, and proclaimed himself king of Scotland.

THE DESPENSERS

Sir Hugh Despenser and his son, also Hugh, were two more of Edward's ill-chosen advisers who incurred the wrath of his opponents because of their mishandling of government. They were both cruelly murdered by Isabella in 1326. Hugh, the younger, was also accused of having a homosexual relationship with the king and was executed by being hanged, drawn, quartered and beheaded (shown left).

BARONS' REBELLION

Edward handed over the running of the country to a handful of favourites, who the barons felt had misgoverned the country. In 1310 they established a committee to try to control the hapless monarch, but to no avail. In 1322 they openly rebelled, led by Thomas, Earl of Lancaster, but the rebellion was defeated. The king was eventually deposed in 1327.

PRINCE OF WALES

Unfortunately, the popular tradition of the infant Edward being held aloft by Edward I in 1284 and presented to the Welsh as a prince, born in Wales but speaking no English, has little basis in fact. Edward was not created Prince of Wales until 1301.

The story was probably English propaganda put about by the Tudors in the 16th century to prove their Welsh ancestry.

Earl of Lancaster, assumes control of government.	to curtail king's powers.	**1314** English defeated by Robert Bruce at the Battle	Thomas, Earl of Lancaster, defeated at Battle of Boroughbridge.	**1327** Edward is formally deposed by Parliament.
1310 Parliament installs Lords Ordainers	**1312** Gaveston captured by king's enemies and executed.	of Bannockburn. **1322** Baron's rebellion, led by	**1326** Edward's wife, Isabella, leaves him for her lover.	**1327** Edward is murdered in Berkeley castle.

⚱ GOVERNMENT   🍵 HEALTH & MEDICINE   ⚖ JUSTICE   ✝ RELIGION   ⧘ SCIENCE

EDWARD III

BORN 1312 • ACCEDED 1327 • DIED 1377

ORDER OF THE GARTER

Edward was the epitome of the medieval, chivalrous king. In 1348 he founded the Order of the Garter, a Chivalric order of knights, based at Windsor Castle, who took their inspiration directly from the epic tales of King Arthur's Knights of the Round Table. In keeping with this general theme, it was during Edward's reign that St. George was proclaimed patron saint of England.

dward came to the throne at the age of 14 in 1327. For the first three years of his reign the country was governed by his mother, Isabella, and her lover, Roger Mortimer. In 1330 Edward seized power for himself and set about righting some of the wrongs that had been directed towards his father. He removed Isabella from office and retired her with a pension, while Mortimer was tried and executed for his crimes. Edward was an heroic figure, like his grandfather, popular with the people because of his just government and victories over France. He was devoted to his wife, Philippa of Hainault, until her death in 1369. He named his new castle and township on the Isle of Sheppey in Kent, Queenborough, in her honour. Edward died eight years after Philippa, it is believed from senile dementia.

THE BLACK PRINCE

Edward III's eldest son, also Edward and known as the Black Prince because of the colour of his armou died the year before his father in 1376 at the age o 46. He won his spurs at the Battle of Crecy in 134 when just 16 years old and soon became the mos feared warrior in Europe. A magnificent effigy of the prince can be seen above his tomb in Canterbury Cathedral.

1327 Edward III becomes king when his father is deposed. **1332** Parliament divided into two separate houses -	Lords and Commons. **1337** Start of '100 Years' War' with France. **1337** Edward claims the	French throne. **1340** Edward defeats French navy at Battle of Sluys. **1346** David II of Scotland	invades England but is defeated at Nevilles's Cross and held prisoner. **1346** French defeated at	Battle of Crécy. **1348** Edward founds chivalri Order of the Garter. **1349/50** Outbreak of Bubonic

🏛 ARCHITECTURE   📖 ARTS & LITERATURE   📜 EXPLORATION   FAMOUS BATTLE

100 YEARS' WAR

Edward claimed the throne of France through his French mother, Isabella, marking the beginning of the 100 Years' War with France. The wars consisted of a series of battles during the period 1337-1453. The English had several early successes, but gradually the tide of the wars changed, with the French finally evicting the English in 1453 at the Battle of Châtillon.

LEGAL REFORMS

Some of the many legal reforms introduced by Edward were the right of Parliament to sanction all tax increases and the Statute of Treason, which for the first time laid down a legal definition as to what did or did not constitute treason.

WINDSOR CASTLE

Edward was born at Windsor Castle, Berkshire, in 1312. The first castle here was of the motte and bailey type and although substantially rebuilt since then it still preserves the typical hour-glass shape of such a castle with its central mound and two courtyards. Edward III transformed e castle into a royal palace from 1346 on. Subsequent monarchs have continued to embellish the buildings which, at nearly 13 acres in extent, form the largest residential castle in the world.

THE BLACK DEATH

The plague, known as the Black Death, is believed to have spread to England sometime in the mid-14th century from the Middle East, though similar diseases may have been around since Saxon times. There were several outbreaks and death was usually swift. Between ⅓ and ⅕ of the population is believed to have died in the 14th century alone. If a similar event occurred in Britain today, with the same ratio of deaths, nearly 20 million people would die.

PARLIAMENT DIVIDED

Edward's military achievements have sometimes eclipsed his prowess as an able and just administrator. He introduced several parliamentary reforms. In 1322 Parliament was divided into two houses, the Lords and the Commons, the former mostly hereditary, the latter elected - much as it is today. This was followed in 1362 by the replacement of French with English as the official language in courts and in parliament.

BATTLE OF CRECY

The Battle of Crecy, near the Somme, was the first major land battle of the 100 Years' War, where a small force of 10,000 English, many of them archers, won a resounding victory over the French. Edward oversaw the battle from a windmill, situated on a nearby hill.

ague (the 'Black Death') decimates the English population.

1351
Statute of Labourers fixes prices

and wages.
1352
Statute of Treason defines exact nature of treasonable offences.

1356
Black Prince defeats French at Battle of Poitiers.
1357
David of Scotland released from prison.

1362
English re-introduced as official language in courts and Parliament, instead of French.

1376
Death of Edward's son, and heir, the Black Prince.
1377
Edward III dies.

🖋 GOVERNMENT   ⚗ HEALTH & MEDICINE   ⚖ JUSTICE   ✝ RELIGION   📜 SCIENCE

RICHARD II

BORN 1367 • ACCEDED 1377 • DEPOSED 1399 • DIED 1400

PEASANTS' REVOLT

The Peasants' Revolt of 1381 was a landmark in English social history, which might have led to open revolution. It was sparked off by the introduction of a poll tax in 1380, levied on individuals equally by the crown, regardless of ability to pay and not related to individual wealth. There were other causes too, in particular the 'Statute of Labourers', which restricted wages and working practices. The 14 year old king faced the rebels and agreed to their demands, but he later reneged on his word and many of the rebels were executed.

WAT TYLER

There were several ringleaders among those involved in the Peasants' Revolt, notably Jack Straw, John Ball and Wat Tyler. Many of the rebels disbanded after meeting Richard, but Tyler led an attack on the Tower of London and killed Simon Sudbury, Archbishop of Canterbury. At a second meeting with the king Tyler was killed by William Walworth, mayor of London.

*R*ichard (the grandson of Edward III) came to the throne at something of a disadvantage. He was a 10 year old boy whose father (the Black Prince) had been a popular hero and he was destined, perhaps, to be ever in his shadow. Until 1389 the country was ruled by advisers. During this time there were several periods of social unrest. Although he ruled well for a while, Richard, a sickly man, was more interested in art and music than government and he became something of a tyrant in later years. He died in prison at just 33 years of age.

CLAIMS TO THE THRONE

Richard II was the son of Edward the Black Prince. Had his father lived he would probably have succeeded to the throne anyway, but when his grandfather Edward III died 1377 there were those who thought the throne should pass to one of his other sons, John of Gaunt. John's son and Richard's cousin - Henry Bolingbroke likewise had a strong claim to the throne, which he exercised when Richard proved incompetent to rule in 1399.

THE KING ABDICATES

Henry Bolingbroke returned from exile in 1399 to reclaim his inheritance. By then Richard, who had been behaving irrationally since the death of his first wife Anne in 1394, had incurred the wrath of his barons. Bolingbroke forced him to abdicate on the grounds of his misrule and imprisoned the king in Pontefract Castle, where he died, suspiciously, a few months later in 1400.

1377 Richard II succeeds his grandfather, Edward III, as king. **1377** Richard's uncles, John of	Gaunt and Thomas of Gloucester, rule England as regents. **1380** John Wycliffe translates New Testament into English.	**1381** Poll Tax introduced, leads to Peasants' Revolt. **1382** Richard marries Anne of Bohemia.	**1387** Lords Appellant take control of government. **1388** Scottish defeat English at Battle of Otterburn in	English borderlands. **1389** Richard resumes control of government. **1390** Robert II of

🏛 ARCHITECTURE   📖 ARTS & LITERATURE   ⚑ EXPLORATION   💣 FAMOUS BATTLE

HENRY YEVELE

nry Yevele was a master mason and director of the king's works, responsible for esigning many royal buildings, such as Westminster Hall. He was the architect rusted by William of Wykeham (Chancellor and Bishop of Winchester) to rebuild e naves of Westminster Abbey and Canterbury Cathedral. He also designed the evolutionary circular castle at Queenborough, in Kent, which is believed to be the first castle built specifically for the use of firearms.

GEOFFREY CHAUCER

Born about 1340, Geoffrey Chaucer earned his living as a soldier, courtier, civil servant and official poet to the court. He became Controller of Customs in London until 1386 and on a diplomatic journey through Italy in 1372 he became familiar with the works of Dante, which influenced his style of writing. His most celebrated work was 'The Canterbury Tales', a narrative story following the journeyings of a group of pilgrims, written sometime between 1387 and his death in 1400.

✝ THE BIBLE TRANSLATED

John Wycliffe was a master of Balliol College, Oxford, where he taught theology and spread his controversial views on church reform. His followers were known as Lollards. He was twice tried for heresy, unsuccessfully, but in 1382 he was finally condemned as a heretic. He escaped execution and retired to Lutterworth (where he translated the Bible into English), until his death in 1384.

JOHN OF GAUNT

ohn of Gaunt (or Ghent, where he was born) was the fourth son of Edward III and accompanied his brother, the Black Prince, on many of his military campaigns. He became the Duke of Lancaster in 1362 and was very influential at court. He acted as mediator etween his nephew, Richard II, and his discontented barons. Relations with the king became strained, however, and Richard exiled John's son, Henry Bolingbroke (later Henry IV) in 1399, when John died, and seized his possessions.

Scotland dies, succeeded by his son, Robert III.	to Ireland. **1396** Richard marries Isabella the king of France's daughter.	**1398** 'Canterbury Tales' published by Geoffrey Chaucer.	**1399** John of Gaunt dies. Henry Bolingbroke becomes Duke of Lancaster.	returns from exile and claims throne.
1394 Richard sends invasion army	**1397** Henry Bolingbroke exiled.	**1399** Richard sets out on second invasion of Ireland.	**1399** Henry Bolingbroke	**1399** Richard II deposed. **1400** Richard dies in prison.

🏛 GOVERNMENT   ⚕ HEALTH & MEDICINE   ⚖ JUSTICE   ✝ RELIGION   📏 SCIENCE

THE SCOTTISH MONARCH

(843-1214)

The early years of the monarchy in Scotland between the years 843-1034, roughly correspond to the period in England where the kings of the seven kingdoms of the Heptarch jostled for power. The Scots, Angles, Picts and Celts were involved in a similar struggle in Scotland. The first king of a united Scotland was Kenneth MacAlpin, a Scot, from whom all the later kings of Scotland claimed to be descended.

YEARS OF TURMOIL

Following the death of Malcolm III in 1093 Scotland underwent a period of considerable change and unrest, coinciding with a Norman invasion from England. Throughout this period, each of the next four Scottish kings tried to counter this invasion by re-asserting their claim to the northernmost counties of England as part of Scotland. Coupled with civil war and a growing period of social unrest, these were turbulent times indeed for Scotland. Malcolm III was succeeded by his brother Donald II in 1093. The following year he was overthrown by his nephew, who had himself crowned as Duncan II. Later that same year he was killed in battle and Donald III returned to the throne, only to be driven off again, on this occasion by Edgar, Duncan's half-brother, in 1097. Edgar ruled until 1107 when he was succeeded by his brother, who became Alexander I.

DUNCAN I (1034-40)

Duncan I succeeded to the throne in 1034 and unsuccessfully launched an invasion of England in 1040. A civil war broke out in Scotland afterwards, during which Duncan was killed. He was succeeded by his cousin, Macbeth.

DAVID I (1124-54)

David succeeded his brother, Alexander I, to the throne in 1124. His long rule of 30 years established a sense of stability to the Scottish throne and h became one of Scotland's ablest rulers. He invited a number of prominent Normans to settle in Scotland and continued to introduce feudalism, althoug the system of government was never fully adopted in Scotland. A pious man, he founded several abbeys and tried unsuccessfully to invade England, being defeated by Stephen at the Battle of the Standard in 1138. David died in 1154 and was succeeded by his grandson, Malcolm IV.

ARCHITECTURE   ARTS & LITERATURE   EXPLORATION   FAMOUS BATTLE

MALCOLM III (1057-93)

Malcolm III took the throne after killing his second cousin, Macbeth. He married Edmund Ironside's granddaughter, Margaret, who was responsible for reforming the Scottish church. William I of England invaded Scotland in 1071-2 and introduced many feudal ideals and forced Malcolm to pay homage to him. Malcolm responded by invading England in 1093 in an attempt to annexe the three northernmost counties to Scotland, but he was killed in the attempt.

WILLIAM THE LION (1165-1214)

William the Lion succeeded his brother, Malcolm IV, to the throne in 1165. In 1173-74 he invaded England but was captured by Henry II in the attempt and surrendered Scottish sovereignty to the English monarch. He purchased Scotland's independence back again in 1189 for a cash payment to Richard I (of England) who was trying to raise money for the crusades. He died in 1214.

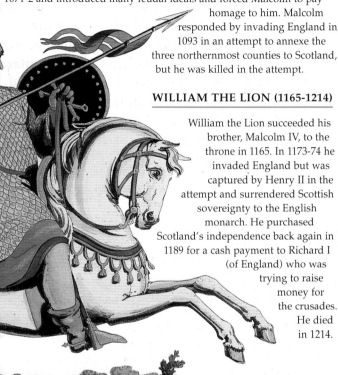

LINE OF SUCCESSION

Early Kings of Scotland

Kenneth MacAlpin - 843-859
Donald I - 859-863
Constantine I - 863-877
Aedh - 877-878
Eocha - 878-889
Donald II - 889-900
Constantine II - 900-942
Malcolm I - 942-954
Indulphus - 954-962
Dubf - 962-967
Cuilean - 967-971
Kenneth II - 971-995
Constantine III - 995-997
Kenneth III - 997-1005
Malcolm II - 1005-1034
Duncan I - 1034-1040
Macbeth - 1040-1057
Malcolm III - 1057-1093
Donald III - 1093-1094 & 1094-1097
Duncan II - 1094
Edgar - 1097-1107
Alexander I - 1107-1124
David I - 1124-1154
Malcolm IV - 1154-1165
William the Lion - 1165-1214

MACBETH (1040-57)

Macbeth came to the throne in 1040 on the death of his cousin, Duncan I. Although implicated with Duncan's death by Shakespeare, there is little evidence to support the claim. It should be pointed out that the 'Duncan' and 'Macbeth' of Shakespeare's play are largely fictitious characters and are not the real kings mentioned here. Macbeth was an able ruler who was killed by Malcolm, Duncan's son, at the Battle of Lumphanan.

GOVERNMENT   HEALTH & MEDICINE   JUSTICE   RELIGION   SCIENCE

NORMAN & PLANTAGENET KINGS & QUEENS OF ENGLAND

THE NORMANS

♛ William I 1066-1087 *m* Matilda of Flanders

♛ William II 1087-1100   ♛ Henry I 1100-1135 *m* Matilda of Scotland   Adela *m* Stephen Count of Blois

Matilda *m* Geoffrey Count of Anjou   ♛ Stephen 1135-1154

THE PLANTAGENETS

♛ Henry II 1154-1189 *m* Elanor of Aquitaine

♛ Richard I 1189-1199   ♛ John 1199-1216 *m* Isabel of Angouleme

♛ Henry II 1216-1272 *m* Elanor of Provence

♛ Edward I 1272-1307 *m* Elanor of Castile

Edward Prince of Wales
(The Black Prince) *m* Joan of Kent   ♛ Edward II 1307-1327 *m* Isabel of France

♛ Richard II 1377-1399   ♛ Edward III 1327-1377 *m* Philippa of Hainault

Although their influence on Anglo-Saxon England was profound, there were in fact only four Norman monarchs to sit on the English throne. In 1035 the Duchy of Normandy passed to William who, in 1066, conquered England. The remainder of the medieval monarchs came from the Plantagenet dynasty, descended from Geoffrey, Count of Anjou, who married Henry I's daughter, Matilda.

ACKNOWLEDGEMENTS

This Series is dedicated to J. Allan Twiggs whose enthusiasm for British History has inspired these four books.
We would also like to thank: Graham Rich, Tracey Pennington, and Peter Done for their assistance.
ticktock Publishing Ltd., The Offices in the Square, Hadlow, Kent TN11 ODD, UK
A CIP Catalogue for this book is available from the British Library. ISBN 1 86007 018 3

Acknowledgements: Picture Credits t=top, b=bottom, c=centre, l=left, r=right, OFC=outside front cover, IFC=inside front cover, IBC=inside back cover, OBC=outside back cover

Ancient Art & Architecture Library: 4tl, 4c, 4bl, 5cl & OBC, 5cr, 8l, 10tl, 12l, 14bc, 15bl, 18tl, 23br, 26tl & bl, 27tl, 28cr, 29cr. Bridgeman Art Library: 5t, 6b, 11cl, 15tl, 16br, 17tl, 21t, 23t & OFC, 29t & IFC. The British Library: 22b. Mary Evans Picture Library: 2tl, 2cl, 2b, 7t, 7b, 8r, 13r & OBC, 15br, 16tl & OFC, 18br & OBC, 19t, 24bl & OBC, 20c, 24bl, 25t, 27l & OBC, 28tl, 30tl &bl, 31tl. Chris Fairclough/Image Select: 6c, 9tr, 11tr, 22t, 27br. Fotomas Index: 12br. Hulton Getty Collection: 14tl. Image Select: 3cl, 13t, 20tl. Kobal Collection: 17br (c Warner Brothers), 31br(c Columbia Pictures). Ann Ronan/Image Select: 24tl, 29tr & ofc cb. David Sellman (c): 10b.

Every effort has been made to trace the copyright holders and we apologise in advance for any unintentional omissions.
We would be pleased to insert the appropriate acknowledgement in any subsequent edition of this publication.
Printed in Italy

A 1,000 YEARS OF BRITISH HISTORY - THE MILLENNIUM SERIES

BOOK I (1,000~1399)   BOOK II (1399~1603)   BOOK III (1603~1714)   BOOK IV (1714~ present day)